PET PALS

Also in the Animal Ark Pets Series

LUCY DANIELS
Pet
Pals

Illustrated by Paul Howard

*Hodder
Children's
Books*

a division of Hodder Headline Limited

Special thanks to Narinder Dhami

Animal Ark is a trademark of Working Partners Limited
Text copyright © 2001 Working Partners Limited,
1 Albion Place, London W6 OQT
Created by Working Partners Limited
Illustrations copyright © 2001 Paul Howard
Cover illustration by Chris Chapman

First published in Great Britain in 2001
by Hodder Children's Books

A Catalogue record for this book is available from the British Library

ISBN 0 340 79558 1

Typeset by Avon Dataset Ltd, Bidford-on-Avon, Warks

Printed and bound in Great Britain by
The Guernsey Press Co. Ltd, Channel Isles

Hodder Children's Books
a division of Hodder Headline Limited
338 Euston Road
London NW1 3BH

Contents

Trio in Trouble

"Hello, Jean." Mandy Hope hurried into the Animal Ark surgery, and smiled at the receptionist, Jean Knox, who was just coming in through the door. It was Saturday morning, and the surgery was just about to open.

"Oh, hello, Mandy," said Jean. She took off her coat and hung it on a peg behind the door. Then she settled down behind the front desk.

"Have Mum and Dad got any of those leaflets

1

left about looking after hamsters?" Mandy asked.

"I'm not sure," Jean replied with a frown. "We ran out so I ordered some more, but I don't know if they've come in yet."

"Sarah Barton in James's class at school has just bought a hamster," Mandy explained, sitting on Jean's desk and swinging her legs to and fro. "I said I'd take one of the leaflets in for her."

Jean winked at Mandy. "Going to make sure she looks after it properly, eh? What a good idea! I'll just go and see if they're in the storeroom."

"Thanks, Jean," Mandy said gratefully.

Sarah had invited Mandy and James to go round to her house, and meet the hamster, who was called Hamish, next week. Mandy was really looking forward to it. She loved hamsters. In fact, she loved *all* animals, so it was great that her mum and dad were both vets. Their surgery, here at Animal Ark, was a modern extension attached to the stone cottage that was their home.

Mandy wondered what pets would be brought into the surgery this morning . . .

Suddenly she jumped as the outside door was pushed open. An elderly woman hurried into the waiting room, looking rather worried. In her arms was a small bundle, wrapped in a tartan blanket.

"Oh!" The woman looked surprised to see Mandy. "I'm sorry. I know I'm rather early for my appointment."

"That's all right," Mandy said politely, sliding off the desk. "The receptionist, Jean, should be back in a minute." She smiled at the woman. "I'm Mandy Hope. My mum and dad are vets here."

"Nice to meet you, dear," the woman replied. "I'm Mrs Green. I've just moved into one of those cottages behind the Fox and Goose pub."

"Welcome to Welford!" Mandy said, smiling. "You'll like it here." Then her curiosity got the better of her. "What's in the blanket, Mrs Green?" she asked.

"Oh, that's Button," Mrs Green said, looking

worried again. She began to unwrap the blanket.

Mandy watched excitedly. A moment later a tiny, furry, tan and white face popped into view. It was a puppy.

"Oh!" she gasped, as Mrs Green unwrapped the blanket a little more. "He's gorgeous. What sort of dog is he?"

"Button's a Pembroke Welsh Corgi," Mrs Green told her. "I've only had him a few days. He's just eight weeks old."

Mandy thought that Button was adorable. He was still quite small, but he had a well-built, sturdy little body, cute perky ears and a tiny stump of a tail. But he didn't look happy at all. He lay listlessly in his owner's arms, looking up at Mandy with sad, dark eyes.

"What's the matter with him?" Mandy asked, gently stroking the puppy's head. "Is he very sick?"

"I just don't know." Mrs Green shrugged. "He seemed miserable as soon as I got him home. And now he won't eat. But I got him from a very well-known breeder in York –

TRIO IN TROUBLE

I'm sure she wouldn't have sold me a sick puppy."

Just then, Mandy's mum, Emily Hope, came into the waiting room. "Mum, this is Mrs Green," Mandy explained. "She's here for the first appointment, with Button."

"So you're taking over Jean's job now, are you?" Mandy's mum teased her. "Hello, Mrs Green. What a beautiful Corgi pup!"

"I just hope you can find out what's wrong with him, Mrs Hope," said Mrs Green anxiously, as Mandy's mum gave the puppy a pat.

"Well, come through and I'll take a look," Emily Hope replied.

"Mum," Mandy began eagerly, as Jean came back with a handful of leaflets, "do you think I could come in and watch?"

"If Mrs Green doesn't mind," her mum answered.

"Of course I don't, dear," the old lady said warmly.

When she'd thanked Jean for the leaflets, Mandy hurried into the surgery after her mum and Mrs Green. Emily Hope had already unwrapped Button, and was checking him over gently. She looked inside his mouth and his ears, examined him all over, listened to his heartbeat and then took his temperature.

"Well?" Mrs Green asked nervously when Mrs Hope had finished.

Mandy felt really sorry for the old lady. She obviously loved her little dog to bits.

Emily Hope frowned. "I can't find anything wrong with him, medically speaking," she said slowly. "But he's definitely under the weather. And I don't like the fact that he's not eating. That's rather worrying."

Mandy bit her lip. Poor little Button looked very small and unhappy, sitting sadly on the examining-table. He didn't seem to be interested in *anything*.

"What shall I do then, Mrs Hope?" asked Mrs Green.

"Try to get Button to eat, if you can," Mandy's mum replied, going over to the sink to wash her hands. "Give him some of his favourite titbits, and keep taking him out for walks and playing with him and so on. Don't treat him too much like an invalid. He might just start to perk up a bit. And bring him back to see me in a week's time."

"'Bye, Button," Mandy whispered, going over to stroke the puppy before Mrs Green wrapped him up in his blanket again. "I hope you feel better soon."

"Well, that was very strange," Mandy's mum remarked, as Mrs Green and Button left the surgery. "That's one very unhappy little puppy, and I have no idea why."

"I hope he starts eating properly soon," Mandy said worriedly.

"Well, dogs have a very strong survival instinct," her mum explained. "So Button won't starve himself for ever, I'm sure. Now, what are you going to do for the rest of the morning?"

"James is coming over," Mandy replied. "We're going to look through my animal books, and find some more information about hamsters for Sarah."

"Ask James to stay for lunch," her mum

suggested, as Mandy went over to the door. "And, Mandy – don't worry about Button. I'm sure he'll be fine."

"OK," Mandy agreed. But she still couldn't get the picture of the Corgi puppy's sad little face out of her mind . . .

"James, listen to this." Mandy was lying on her tummy on the living-room carpet, leafing through one of her many animal books. "It says here that according to old Welsh legends, the fairies and elves used to ride on them."

"What, *hamsters*?" James asked, his eyes round behind his glasses.

"No, silly!" Mandy laughed. "Corgi dogs!" She'd told James all about Button as soon as he'd arrived.

"Really?" James came over to look at the book too. "I didn't know Corgis came from Wales."

Mandy nodded. "They're pretty special dogs," she smiled. "Even the Queen has some of them."

"I wonder why Button is so unhappy?" James

said thoughtfully. "Maybe Mrs Green isn't looking after him properly."

Mandy shook her head. "No, I don't think it's that. Mrs Green really loves Button, I could tell." Then she glanced at the clock. "Mum should be finishing morning surgery now. Shall we go in and see her?"

James nodded, so they went through into Animal Ark. Jean was busy at her desk with a young man who was paying his bill, so they didn't go over to say hello.

"The examination room's door is closed," Mandy said, nudging James. "Mum must still be with her last patient."

But at that very moment, the door opened. Mandy's eyes widened in surprise as *Button* trotted out!

"James," she began eagerly, "that's—"

But then she stopped. The woman who was following him out, holding the puppy's lead, wasn't Mrs Green. It was another elderly lady, much shorter and plumper than Button's owner.

"That looks like a Corgi puppy," James

whispered to Mandy. "Is it Button?"

"Well, it certainly looks like him, but I don't think it can be," Mandy whispered back. She was completely confused. She hadn't seen a Corgi puppy at Animal Ark before today, and now here were two in one morning!

Mandy's mum had followed the woman and the puppy out of the surgery. She saw Mandy and James staring, and beckoned them over.

"No, Mandy, you're not seeing things!" she laughed. "This isn't Button. Her name's Meg,

and she's exactly the same age as Mrs Green's pup. Meg belongs to Miss Daniels, who's come over from Walton."

Miss Daniels smiled at Mandy and James. "Do you like Corgi pups?" she asked.

"Oh, yes," Mandy replied, getting down on her hands and knees to say hello to Meg. The puppy sniffed her hand and let Mandy and James stroke her, but she didn't really seem very interested. She sat at her owner's feet, her perky little ears drooping miserably.

"She doesn't seem very happy," James said.

"No, she isn't," Miss Daniels sighed. "Well, I'll try what you suggested, Mrs Hope, and I'll see you again in a week's time." And she went over to see Jean to make an appointment.

"Mum, Meg seems to be very sad, just like Button," Mandy remarked, as they followed Mrs Hope back into the surgery.

Mandy's mum sighed. "Yes, she is." She sprayed the examination-table with disinfectant, and began to wipe it down. "They're both not eating, they're both very miserable . . . I just don't know what's wrong."

"Maybe Dad will have some ideas," Mandy suggested hopefully.

"True," her mum agreed. "We'll ask him when he gets back from shopping in Walton."

Mr Hope didn't arrive home until lunch was almost ready. Mandy and James were watching for him impatiently, and they ran out to help him with the shopping when he began unloading it from Animal Ark's Land-rover.

"Dad, we need to ask you something," Mandy began.

Her father groaned. "Don't tell me!" he said teasingly. "It's about an animal, isn't it?"

Mandy grinned. "What else?" she said, and she quickly told her father all about Button and Meg.

"And we were wondering if you had any idea what could be wrong with them," she finished.

Mr Hope was looking very thoughtful. "It's funny you should say that," he murmured with a frown, as they carried the bags of shopping inside. "As a matter of fact, I heard something very similar the other day . . ."

13

"What?" Mandy and James asked eagerly.

Mrs Hope, who'd heard them come in, hurried over to listen too.

"A friend of mine who's a vet in York rang me for some advice," Mandy's dad went on. "He'd just seen an eight-week-old Corgi pup who was really miserable and off his food, and he didn't know what was wrong with it—"

"Just like Button and Meg!" Mandy interrupted.

Her dad nodded.

"So what did you say?" James asked eagerly.

Mr Hope shrugged. "I told my friend I didn't have a clue what was wrong with it either!" he said ruefully.

Mandy and James's faces fell.

"Oh, *Dad*!" Mandy sighed. "I thought you were going to give us the answer." Then all of a sudden, her face lit up. "I've just thought of something!" she exclaimed.

"What?" James asked curiously.

"Well, Button and Meg and the puppy Dad's friend saw are *all* the same age, and *all* from York. Maybe they're from the same litter."

Mandy was so excited, the words tumbled out at top speed. "Maybe they're brothers and sisters, and they've all got the same problem!" she finished.

"It's possible," Emily Hope agreed, glancing at her husband. "Corgi pups aren't that common. There can't be many breeders in York with a litter born just over eight weeks ago. So it's quite possible that they all came from the same litter."

She got up and headed for the Animal Ark surgery. "I'll call Miss Daniels and Mrs Green, and find out *exactly* where the puppies came from," she said. "I'll have to look up their numbers in the files."

"And I'll ring my friend Graham in York," Mr Hope added, going to the telephone in the hall.

James looked rather puzzled, and nudged Mandy. "I don't understand," he whispered. "How will it help to know if they're all from the same litter?"

"Well, if they're *all* sick, it might be something they got from their mother," Mandy explained. "Then the breeder might be able to help."

"Oh, I see." James nodded.

They stood and waited impatiently while Mandy's dad chatted to his friend for a while. When he came off the phone he'd found out that the puppy's name was Jasper, and his owner was called Mrs Reid. He'd also written down the name of the breeder Mrs Reid had bought Jasper from. It was a woman called Mrs Whitehouse who lived in York.

"Do you know her, Dad?" Mandy asked.

Mr Hope nodded. "Yes, she's been breeding Corgis for years. And I'm sure she wouldn't have sold three sickly puppies. No well-known breeder would do such thing."

At that moment Mandy's mum came out of the surgery. "Button and Meg came from the same breeder," she said triumphantly. "Mrs Whitehouse in York."

"So Button and Meg and Jasper are *all* from the same litter!" James gasped. "Well done, Mandy!" And he patted her on the back.

Mandy turned pink. "Did you ring Mrs

Whitehouse, Mum?" she asked.

"I tried, but she was out," Mrs Hope replied.

"OH!" Mandy said suddenly. She hadn't meant to say it *quite* so loudly, but another idea had just popped into her head. "Mum, Dad, do you think Button, Jasper and Meg could be *missing* each other?"

The others stared at her.

"You mean they might not be ill? They could just be pining for each other?" James asked.

Mandy nodded eagerly. "And that might be

why they're off their food," she went on.

Mr and Mrs Hope looked at each other thoughtfully.

"That idea is certainly worth investigating," Mr Hope said approvingly.

"Well spotted, love!" Mrs Hope said, giving her a hug.

Mandy felt a warm glow of happiness. "Maybe the puppies and their owners could all get together," she suggested. "Then we could see if the pups feel better."

Mr Hope nodded. "We'll have to talk to the owners about that," he said. "But it's a good idea, Mandy."

Mandy grinned. She might just have made three sad little Corgi puppies very happy . . .

Over the next week, Mr and Mrs Hope contacted the breeder, Mrs Whitehouse, who confirmed that there was nothing wrong with the pups' mother. Mrs Whitehouse also said that the three puppies had been particularly close, and that she had hated having to split them up.

"It looks as if you could be right, Mandy," Mrs Hope said, when she'd finished talking to Mrs Whitehouse. "The puppies might well be missing each other."

"So what happens now?" asked Mandy.

"We just have to hope they settle down with their new owners," Mandy's dad replied.

"Mandy, I think you and James ought to take a walk to the village green," Mr Hope remarked, popping his head round the surgery door. It was the following Saturday, and Mandy and James were sitting in the waiting room.

"But, Dad, we're waiting to see Meg and Button," Mandy protested. "Mum told them to come back today for a check-up."

Mandy was longing to see if the two Corgi puppies were any better.

"Button and Meg won't be coming to Animal Ark today," Mr Hope replied, looking as if he was trying not to smile. "I really do think you two should get along to the village green instead of waiting here . . ." he added.

"What's going on, Dad?" Mandy asked curiously.

But Mr Hope shook his head. "My lips are sealed!" he said mysteriously. "Off you go."

Puzzled, Mandy and James reluctantly left the surgery, and walked through Welford to the village green.

"Why on earth did Dad want to get rid of us?" Mandy wondered. "And why does he want us to go to the green?"

"If I'd known we were coming out, I'd have brought Blackie with me," James added. "I left him at home because I didn't want him running round turning Animal Ark upside-down!"

The green was just in front of them now. Suddenly Mandy stopped dead in her tracks, and gasped, putting her hand to her mouth. "James, look!" she cried.

The village green seemed to be alive with Corgi puppies! There were *three* of them running around on their leads, all with almost exactly the same tan and white markings.

"That's Button and Mrs Green!" Mandy said,

hardly able to believe her eyes.

"And that's Meg and Miss Daniels!" James gasped.

"So the third puppy must be Jasper, and that must be his owner, Mrs Reid," Mandy guessed. "Come on, James!"

The two of them raced across the green towards the Corgi pups and their three elderly owners. The pups caught sight of them, and began to jump around barking gleefully, looking delighted to see some new friends.

"Hello, Button," Mandy laughed, bending down to ruffle the puppy's thick fur. The change in both Button and Meg, who was also begging for Mandy's attention, was quite amazing. They were now bright-eyed and lively, and full of beans. "Hello, Mrs Green, hello, Miss Daniels."

"Letty, this is the young girl we were telling you about." Mrs Green turned to Jasper's owner, Mrs Reid. "She was the one who realised the pups were missing each other."

Mandy blushed, as Mrs Reid looked at her gratefully.

"Thank you so much, dear," she said. "I was so worried about Jasper. I couldn't think what on earth was wrong with him."

"There's not much wrong with the three of them now!" Miss Daniels laughed. They all looked down at Mandy who was still kneeling on the grass, trying to cuddle all three lively puppies at once.

"And, Mandy, we're going to make sure the puppies meet up regularly," Mrs Green explained. "We're all retired, so we have plenty of time to visit each other."

"That's great," Mandy said happily.

"It looks as if Mrs Reid, Mrs Green and Miss Daniels are going to be as good friends as the puppies are!" James whispered to Mandy.

"I hope so," Mandy laughed, looking round at the three almost-identical pups. "I just hope they don't get the dogs mixed up, that's all!"

Harold's Hideaway

"Look at this, Mandy!" James gazed at the large pile of clothes heaped on the sofa in the sitting room of Lilac Cottage. "The guy will be the best-dressed person in Welford on Bonfire Night!"

Mandy grinned at her gran. "Thanks for finding all this stuff," she said.

"Well, they're only old things of Grandad's that he's been hanging on to," Gran said with a smile. "To be honest, I've been looking for a chance to get rid of them."

"I heard that," Grandad Hope snorted, coming into the sitting room. "I expect my favourite gardening trousers are in that pile somewhere!"

"Go on with you!" Gran scolded him, but her eyes were twinkling. "The guy wouldn't want to wear those dirty old things – no one would, except you!"

Mandy and James laughed, and Blackie, who was lying in front of the fire, joined in by barking loudly.

"Gran, shall we take these clothes round to Mary now?" Mandy asked. Mary was a good friend of Gran and Grandad Hope. They often looked after her Russian hamster, Frisky, when she was on holiday. Mary lived at Cowslip Cottage on Hobart's Corner, and the village Bonfire Night celebrations were taking place in the field behind her house the following evening. This year, Mary had volunteered to make the guy to go on top of the bonfire.

Gran nodded. "Yes, I'll just pop them into some plastic bags for you." She hurried out to the kitchen, and returned with a black bin-bag. "Do you want to come back here for lunch afterwards?"

"Yes, please!" James said eagerly, then blushed. He was a big fan of Mandy's gran's cooking.

"It's casserole with dumplings, and toffee pudding for afters," Gran added, and Mandy and James cheered.

"Brr, it's freezing," Mandy said, as she and James left Lilac Cottage, carrying the bag of clothes. She wound her long, stripy scarf round her neck more tightly. "I wonder if Harold's gone into hibernation yet?"

Harold was a hedgehog who lived in Mary's garden. Earlier that year, his nest under the apple tree had been flooded, and Harold had disappeared. Mandy and James had been very worried, especially when they found the hedgehog half-frozen and in shock. But thanks to Mandy's mum, he had pulled through, and was now living happily in the garden of Cowslip Cottage again.

"Sorry?" James wasn't listening. He was too

busy trying to control Blackie, who was bounding along the pavement. "Blackie, stop it!"

"Well, now, I think the guy is going to have a very difficult time deciding what to wear!" Mary declared with a smile, as she opened her front door to find Mandy, James and Blackie standing there with the big bag of clothes. "Come in, do. You must be half-frozen."

Mandy and James hurried inside Cowslip Cottage gratefully. Mary had a roaring fire in the grate, and it was warm and cosy inside the little house. Blackie immediately made for the hearthrug, and settled down to toast his paws.

"Hello, Frisky." Mandy went over to see the hamster, who was in his cage on the sideboard. Frisky was curled up, snugly, in the nest he had built and was fast asleep, although when he heard Mandy's voice, he poked his little nose out and looked at her with his shiny black eyes. Then he yawned and curled up again.

"Well, what do you think?" Mary was standing in the doorway, holding the guy. She wasn't very tall, and the guy was much bigger than she was! It was made of white cotton material, stuffed with old rags, and looked rather strange because it didn't have any clothes on, and Mary hadn't painted its face on yet.

"He's fantastic!" James said admiringly. "Isn't he, Mandy?"

Mandy nodded. "He's the biggest guy we've ever had," she said.

Mary laid the guy carefully on the sofa. "Do you two want to help me dress him, and paint his face on?" she asked.

"Yes, please," Mandy said eagerly.

"Don't forget we're having lunch at your gran's," James reminded her.

Mandy laughed. "Don't worry, James," she told him. "We've got plenty of time."

Mary emptied the bag of clothes on to the floor. "Let's make sure we wrap him up warmly," she said, her eyes twinkling. "It's going to be very cold on top of that bonfire!"

"Gosh, it's a huge bonfire this year!" Mandy said, as she gazed out over Mary's back garden. She could see the field beyond it, with the bonfire in the middle. It was made up of tree branches, large bits of wood, and old furniture.

Suddenly Mandy gave a gasp. She'd just spotted something moving in Mary's garden. "James, come and look!" she called. "It's Harold!"

James hurried over to the window. Together they watched Harold snuffling his way along Mary's lawn, his bright dark eyes searching from side to side. The hedgehog looked plump and healthy, and his spikes gleamed in the pale sunshine, as he picked his way over to one of the flowerbeds on his tiny brown paws.

"He's getting ready to hibernate," Mary remarked, coming to look over their shoulders. "So he's looking for lots of slugs and beetles to fatten himself up a bit more."

"I wonder where he'll sleep this time," Mandy said.

"Maybe he'll go back to his old nest in the roots of the apple tree," James suggested.

Mary shook her head. "No. Hedgehogs never use the same nest twice," she explained.

"But there are plenty of other places for him to choose."

Mandy watched the hedgehog until he disappeared out of sight behind a bush. "Good luck, Harold," she whispered. "I hope you find a warm and cosy place to make your nest . . ."

"Not long to go now!" Mandy said eagerly, as she and James walked up the path to Cowslip Cottage. It was the following morning, and they were visiting Mary again to help her with the final preparations for Bonfire Night. The guy's face was only half-painted, and they'd also promised to help Mary scrub piles and piles of potatoes, so that they could be baked in the fire. "I can't *wait* till tonight."

"Me neither," James agreed. "I hope the fireworks are as good as they were last year."

"Remember to keep Benji and Blackie safely locked in the house tonight, won't you?" Mandy reminded him anxiously, glancing down at the Labrador puppy who was trotting along next to them.

"Don't worry," James replied, knocking on Mary's door. "I won't forget."

When Mary opened the door, Mandy was surprised to see that the elderly lady looked rather upset. "What's the matter, Mary?" she asked, quickly.

"It's Harold," Mary explained. "I can't find him anywhere."

"Well, maybe he's hibernated by now," Mandy said, trying to comfort her.

"Yes, but where?" said Mary, worriedly.

"I've searched the whole garden, and I can't see his nest anywhere."

"Mandy and I could look for him," James suggested.

Mary brightened up a little. "Oh, would you?" she said eagerly. "I'm cooking soup for tonight, and I can't really leave it."

"We'll have a good look," Mandy told her. "And Blackie can help us."

Mary hurried back into the kitchen while Mandy, James and Blackie went round to the back garden.

"I wonder where Harold's nest could be," Mandy said thoughtfully. Like Mary, she was worried about the hedgehog, but she knew that Harold was fit and healthy. Still, it would be much safer to know where his nest was, just in case there was another flood or some other kind of disaster.

"Let's look under the roots of the apple tree first," James suggested. "He *might* have gone back to it."

James and Mandy hurried to the apple tree at the bottom of the garden, but Harold wasn't there, and there was no sign of a nest. Next, they looked in Mary's compost heap. Mandy knew that hedgehogs loved to bury themselves right out of sight, and Harold had lived in her grandad's compost heap after his first nest had been flooded. Blackie helped by digging away at the compost, but there was still no sign of him.

After that they searched Mary's woodshed, and then looked all round the garden. They checked under every bush, but the hedgehog seemed to have vanished into thin air.

"Did you find him?" Mary asked anxiously, when Mandy and James went inside again.

Mandy shook her head sadly.

"Oh, dear," Mary said, with a little catch in her voice. "I hope he hasn't moved into someone else's garden. I've got so used to having him around."

Mandy glanced at James. It *did* seem the most likely explanation. But Harold had seemed so happy in Mary's garden. Why would he have moved?

★ ★ ★

"Come on, Mandy," Emily Hope called up the stairs. "The bonfire is being lit in ten minutes, and they'll start the fireworks soon after that. We don't want to miss any!"

"Coming!" Mandy called back, as she pulled on a sweater. She had been looking forward to Bonfire Night so much, but now she felt too worried about Harold to be excited about the bonfire display. Mary was obviously worried too, although she had tried to be cheerful while they finished painting the guy's face. Mandy

35

and James had gone back into the garden to have another look for Harold before they'd left, but there was still no sign of the missing hedgehog.

Mandy grabbed her thick coat, and hurried downstairs. Her mum was waiting for her by the door. "Where's Dad?" she asked.

"He's just coming," Mrs Hope replied.

Mandy's mum and dad had been out all day, visiting friends who lived in York, and they'd only just got back. Mandy had spent the day with Gran and Grandad, and had only just come home herself to change into some warmer clothes, so she hadn't had a chance to tell her mum and dad about Harold yet.

"Did you have a good day, love?" Mrs Hope asked her. "Did you finish the guy?"

"Yes, we did," Mandy began, "but Mary is really worried about Harold—"

At that moment Adam Hope clattered down the stairs, pulling on his jacket. "Let's go!"

"What were you saying about Harold, love?" her mum asked, as they left the house and walked down the lane.

"Mary's really worried because Harold's hibernated, and she can't find his nest," Mandy replied. "She thinks he might have moved into someone else's garden."

"Well, it's certainly possible," Mr Hope said absent-mindedly.

"We finished the guy and everything's ready," Mandy went on. "But I just can't stop thinking about Harold."

Her father stopped still in his tracks. "What did you say just then, Mandy?"

"Just that I can't stop thinking about Harold," Mandy repeated.

"No, the other bit . . . about the guy," Mr Hope said.

"Well, just that we finished it," Mandy began, looking puzzled. She jumped as her father grabbed her hand.

"Quick, into the Land-rover!" he said urgently. "We need to get a move on. Luckily I've got the keys in my pocket."

"But I thought we were walking—" Mrs Hope began.

"No time," Mr Hope said, unlocking

the car. "Come on, get in."

"Dad, what's the matter?" Mandy asked, confused, as he revved up the engine.

"I think I know where Harold might have built his nest," her father replied.

"Where?" Mandy was still puzzled.

"In the bonfire," Adam Hope said grimly.

"Oh no!" Mandy gasped in horror. She hadn't thought of that. But she knew that people were often warned to check their bonfires, in case a hedgehog had crawled inside.

"Quick, Adam," Emily Hope urged him. "The bonfire is being lit in less than five minutes!"

Mandy's heart pounded with fear, as they drove through Welford to Hobart's Corner. She kept glancing at the clock on the dashboard. Would they be in time to save Harold?

As they jumped out of the car behind Mary's house, Mandy's heart began to pound again, but this time with relief. The bonfire stood, tall and dark, with the guy perched on top, still waiting to be lit. The area around the bonfire was roped off, and there were crowds of people behind the barriers. There was a buzz of excited chatter, as everyone waited.

"Look, Dad!" Mandy said urgently, grabbing her father's arm. She had spotted Mary, standing by the bonfire with a lighted taper in her hand. Mandy's grandad was with her, and he was holding a taper too. "They're going to light it!" she gasped.

Mr Hope cupped his hands round his mouth and yelled "Mary! Wait!"

To Mandy's enormous relief, Mary heard him over the buzz of the crowd, and looked up. She waved. "You're just in time," she called. "We're about to light the bonfire."

"No, not yet," Mr Hope called back, and hurried over to her. Meanwhile Mandy's gran and James had appeared out of the crowd.

"What's going on?" James asked curiously, and Mandy quickly explained. Then they all hurried over to Mary and Mr Hope.

"Oh, my goodness." Mary had turned quite pale. "Do you really think he might be in there?

We'd better have a good look."

So Mandy, her parents, her grandparents, and James and Mary began to search around the bottom of the bonfire. News had got round about Harold and the crowd fell silent as everyone watched them.

There were lots of pieces of screwed-up newspaper stuffed into the bottom of the bonfire so that the fire would catch light easily. Mandy and James knelt down and carefully checked through them to make sure that Harold wasn't underneath.

As Mandy was about to stand up to check a different part of the fire, she blinked. Was it her imagination, or had that bundle of newspaper and leaves just moved?

She stretched out her hand and touched it gently. There was something prickly and heavy inside! "Dad!" she yelled excitedly. "I think I've found him!"

Adam Hope raced over to Mandy as she lifted the bundle out of the bonfire, and laid it carefully on the grass. She opened it up gently with trembling hands, while everyone stood around watching – and there was Harold, still rolled up in a tight ball, fast asleep! "Oh, thank goodness he's safe!" Mandy gasped.

A cheer went up from the crowd.

"Let's get the little fellow away from here before he wakes up," Mandy's dad suggested. "What about putting him in your woodshed, Mary?"

"Good idea," Mary agreed, looking very relieved that Harold had been found safe and sound.

Between them Mandy and James carried Harold's nest carefully across the field to Mary's woodshed, and put it in a dark corner. Then they covered it with an old sack.

"He'll be quite safe there," Adam Hope said with a smile.

"Goodnight, Harold," Mandy said. "See you in the spring!"

By the time they made their way back to the field, Mandy's grandad had lit the bonfire, and the flames were already beginning to catch and burn.

"This is a brilliant Bonfire Night!" James said to Mandy, as the first firework whooshed its way into the sky and burst into a shower of glittering sparks.

"Yes, it is," Mandy agreed. "And best of all, Harold's now safely tucked up for the winter in his hedgehog home!"

A New Home

"Oh, look, Dad!" Mandy exclaimed in delight. She was watching a newborn foal stand for the first time. The foal's spindly legs were a bit shaky, but she managed it at last. Then she trotted over to her mother, who bent her large, shaggy head down, and nuzzled her gently.

Mandy sighed. "Isn't she lovely?"

"She's a beauty," Mr Hope agreed with a smile, putting his medical bag down on the stable floor.

"What are you going to call her, Mr Bromyard?" Mandy asked, turning to the elderly farmer.

"Venus," Mr Bromyard replied. "She's a lively one, isn't she?" he added, as Venus gazed curiously at the visitors with big brown eyes.

Mandy and her father had come to Peak Farm so that Mr Hope could check up on Venus and her mum, Juno, after the birth.

"Can I stroke Venus?" Mandy asked, looking first at Mr Bromyard and then her dad.

"Yes, but be careful, and stay outside the stall," her father told her, as he took off his jacket and rolled up his sleeves. "You know how new mums can be a little nervous."

Mandy nodded. She leaned over as quietly as she could and patted the foal's fluffy neck. Juno swished her long tail, but she didn't seem to mind.

"Juno, Venus and Apollo are Clydesdale horses, aren't they, Mr Bromyard?" Mandy asked. "They look like Shire horses, but a bit smaller." Apollo was Venus's father, a beautiful, black stallion. Both of the parents had sleek coats with long manes and shaggy hooves, but the foal's coat was still fuzzy.

"That's right," Mr Bromyard replied. "We've always had Clydesdales on Peak Farm." He suddenly looked sad. "But not for much longer, I'm afraid."

"Why not?" Mandy asked, surprised.

Mr Bromyard looked even more miserable. "I have to find new homes for Apollo, Juno and Venus very soon," he explained. "The horses haven't worked on the farm for the last few years, since my son Nick took over running it, and they're becoming too expensive to look after."

"Some farmers keep Clydesdales just for showing at agricultural shows or breeding, not for working on the farm," Mr Hope pointed out. "Couldn't they pay their way if you did that?"

"I've thought about it," Mr Bromyard admitted. "But I'm getting on a bit, and it would be a lot of hard work."

Mandy felt a big lump rise in her throat as she looked at Juno and her foal. They looked so peaceful and cosy in their stall. But what would happen to them now?

"Mr Bromyard, will they all be able to go to the same home?" she asked anxiously. "I'm sure they'd want to stay together."

The old farmer scratched his head. "There's nothing I'd like more, lass, but I'm not sure if it's possible," he replied. "I've asked around, and no one seems interested in taking all three of them."

"What about Joyce Dawkins at the Glisterdale Horse and Pony Rescue Centre?" Mandy suggested hopefully.

"I've already asked her," Mr Bromyard sighed. "She can take Juno and Venus, but not Apollo. She would need to keep a stallion away from her other mares and she hasn't got the space."

Mandy bit her lip. She went over to the stable door, and looked out across the farmyard. In a nearby field, Apollo was cantering up and down, tossing his long mane, his black coat gleaming in the sunshine.

"There must be *someone* who can look after

all three of them," she muttered, racking her brains.

"Isn't there anyone who'd like them as working horses?" Adam Hope asked. "I know everything's done by machine now, but surely there must be people who want to keep the old ways of farming alive."

"An agricultural museum might be interested," Mr Bromyard agreed. "But there aren't any round here."

"What kind of work did the horses do on the farm?" Mandy asked.

"Well, they were mostly used for pulling carts and for ploughing," Mr Bromyard explained. "Come and look at this."

The farmer led Mandy and Mr Hope outside, and over to a large piece of machinery, which was covered with tarpaulin. He lifted a corner of it, and showed them a shiny, old-fashioned plough. "That's the plough my grandfather used to dig the fields years ago," he said proudly. "And it was pulled by Clydesdales. I've spent hours restoring the plough to its original condition."

"What are you going to do with it?" Mr Hope asked.

"Give it to a museum, I suppose." Mr Bromyard looked glum again. "I'd be happy to see the horses and the plough go to someone who'd actually use them to demonstrate ploughing at agricultural shows, but there's no one round here who seems to want them. Still, there's not a lot we can do about that." Sadly, he turned and made his way back to the stables.

"Mandy, you've got that look in your eye again!" her father teased, as they walked across the yard. "If I know you, you're going to find a new home for Venus and her parents!"

Mandy glanced back over her shoulder at Apollo, who was now grazing peacefully, and then into the stables at Juno and Venus. The foal was cuddled close against her mother's side.

"Well, I'm certainly going to do my best, Dad," she said in a determined voice.

"Look, Mandy, here's some information about Clydesdales." James passed her the book he'd been looking at.

"Oh, great." Mandy took it, and read the page quickly. "It says that Clydesdales are quite a rare breed," she told James. "There's not that many of them left."

"Oh, well, at least Venus makes one more!" James said, pushing his glasses up his nose. He'd come round to the Hopes' house for lunch, and Mandy had told him all about the family of Clydesdales at Peak Farm, and how Mr Bromyard was searching for a new home for them.

"It says here that black Clydesdales are quite rare." Mandy stared at the big picture in the middle of the page. "That looks just like Apollo."

"Why do they have so much hair at the bottom of their legs?" James wanted to know.

"I think it helps to protect their legs and feet," Mandy replied. "Look, this brown-and-white one looks like Juno."

James whistled. "A Clydesdale's hoof is as big as a football," he read out, "only a lot heavier." He grinned at Mandy. "They must be seriously *big*!"

"Yes, which means they're quite expensive to feed and look after." Mandy sighed.

Just then, Mr Hope popped his head round the door. "I have to go over to Woodbridge Farm Park," he said. "One of their sheep has gone lame. Do you two want to come along?"

Woodbridge Farm Park, which was just outside Welford, used to be an ordinary working farm, but now it was open to the public. Mandy and James had been there several times when they were doing school projects.

"Yes, please," Mandy said, scrambling to her feet. Then a sudden thought struck her. "Maybe Mr Marsh will know someone who wants Mr Bromyard's horses." Mr Marsh was the farm park manager.

"He might do," her father agreed, as they went out to the Land-rover.

"Maybe the horses could live at Woodbridge Farm Park," James suggested hopefully.

Mandy's face lit up. "That's a good idea, James!" she began, but her father was already shaking his head.

"I don't think so, love. After all, the horses wouldn't be doing anything. They'd just be there for the public to see, not earning their keep like other animals on the farm."

"I bet people would love to see them though," Mandy pointed out.

"Yes, but it would be very expensive for Mr

Woodbridge," her father said gently. Mr
Woodbridge was the owner of the farm. "He
couldn't afford to have the horses sitting round
doing nothing."

Mandy knew her dad was right, but it didn't
make her feel any better. She sat in silence on
the journey to the farm park, thinking about
Venus, Juno and Apollo. There just *had* to be
a good home waiting for all three of them
somewhere . . .

Mr Hope drove down the long track which
led to Woodbridge Farm Park. There were
quite a few visitors wandering around, looking
at the animals. The farm had a herd of Jersey
cows, a flock of sheep and some pigs, including
Sally the sow, as well as geese, hens and ducks.

Mr Marsh was waiting outside the large barn,
which was used as a refreshments area,
watching out for them. "Thanks for coming
so quickly, Adam," he said, as they shook
hands. "I'm a bit worried about this sheep.
She can hardly walk." He smiled at Mandy
and James. "Hello, you two."

Mr Hope turned to Mandy and James. "Why don't you stay here and say hello to the animals?" he suggested. "I'll come and find you when I've finished."

They nodded, quite happy to do that.

"Let's go to the pigsty, and say hello to Sally," James suggested.

"OK," Mandy agreed, glancing round the farm. There were so many fields all around, it would be a perfect home for the three Clydesdale horses. But she knew her dad was right. The horses wouldn't be able to earn their keep.

"What are you reading, James?" Mandy asked, noticing that he was studying a poster pinned on the barn door.

"Oh, there's a spinning demonstration here next weekend," James replied. "Look." He pointed at the picture on the poster, which was of an old-fashioned spinning wheel. "They're going to use wool from the Woodbridge sheep."

"Oh!" Mandy gasped, looking excited.

"What's up?" James asked, puzzled.

But before Mandy could reply, the owner of

the farm, Mr Woodbridge, walked out of the barn. "Hello, Mandy, hello, James," he said cheerfully. He was a tall, friendly-looking man. "Nice to see you again."

"Hello, Mr Woodbridge," Mandy said breathlessly. "We were just looking at this poster about the spinning demonstration."

"Ah, yes." The farmer smiled. "This is the first one we've ever done, but people seem really interested in those old farming skills."

"Have you ever thought about doing any

54

other demonstrations?" Mandy asked, her heart thumping.

"What do you mean?" Mr Woodbridge looked confused.

"Well, like ploughing with Clydesdale horses, for instance," Mandy suggested. James grinned.

Mr Woodbridge stroked his chin. "That's interesting . . . But I'm not sure we could afford to keep Clydesdales on the farm."

"You could if they were doing ploughing demonstrations all the time," Mandy said eagerly. Her mind raced as she tried to think of other good reasons. "And they're good at pulling carts, so they could give rides to the public too," she added breathlessly. "*And* they're not as big as Shire horses, so they're cheaper to feed."

Mr Woodbridge's eyes twinkled. "I think you've got some particular horses in mind, haven't you, Mandy Hope?"

Quickly Mandy explained about Venus, Apollo and Juno.

When she mentioned that Apollo was a black stallion, Mr Woodbridge looked very interested. "Hmm, I've been thinking about starting to breed rare types of farm animals," he said thoughtfully. "It's important not to let the unusual breeds die out."

Mandy and James grinned delightedly at each other, just as Mr Hope and Mr Marsh came over to them. "So you'll think about it?" Mandy asked, her heart thumping.

"Better than that," Mr Woodbridge replied. "I'll go over and see Mr Bromyard right away."

"You've got a very good saleswoman for a daughter, Adam!" said Mr Woodbridge with a smile. "I think Woodbridge Farm Park has just found itself three Clydesdale horses!"

"Well!" said Mr Bromyard, staring at Mr Woodbridge in surprise. "I never expected this. But of course I'm happy to let the horses go to Woodbridge Farm Park. I know how well you look after your animals."

Mandy beamed happily.

"It was all Mandy's idea," Mr Woodbridge explained. "The horses will be a big attraction at the farm, especially if they're doing ploughing demonstrations and giving rides. I'm sure they'll earn their keep."

"Thanks, Mandy," Mr Bromyard said gratefully, and Mandy blushed. "Adam, you've got a very clever daughter."

"And a determined one!" Mr Hope smiled, putting his arm round Mandy's shoulders.

"There's just one problem," Mr Woodbridge began. Mandy's heart sank. "Neither my farm manager nor I have ever ploughed with horses before!"

"Oh, don't worry," Mr Bromyard said. "I'll teach you. I'll even give you my old plough."

"Thanks very much," Mr Woodbridge replied, looking relieved. "Perhaps you'd like to come and give ploughing demonstrations yourself sometimes? After all, you're the expert!"

Mr Bromyard looked delighted. "I'd love to," he said warmly. "I wouldn't like to lose touch with my horses altogether."

Mandy looked at Apollo, who was wandering peacefully around his field. Then she slipped over to the doorway of the stables, and gazed in at the tiny foal, Venus, and her mum, Juno. "You're all going to stay together and be a real family," Mandy whispered softly. "Good luck in your new home!"

Guinea-pigs Galore!

"Mrs Todd, Lisa's here with the baby guinea-pigs!" Mandy said excitedly to her teacher. "Shall I give her a hand?"

It was the beginning of the day at Welford Primary School, and the bell had just rung. Everyone else was on their way into class, but Mandy had spotted the Glovers' car pulling up outside the school gates. Today, Lisa was bringing in Carla, her guinea-pig, and Carla's three new babies. Mandy couldn't wait to see them.

"All right, Mandy," Mrs Todd agreed, as Lisa climbed out of the car, holding the guinea-pigs' cage.

Mandy rushed across the playground. "Hi, Lisa," she called. "Let me give you a hand."

"Thanks, Mandy," said Lisa gratefully, handing over her school bag. "Do you want to have a look at the babies?"

"You bet!" Mandy grinned. She peered into the cage. There was Carla, who was a beautiful tortoiseshell–and–white, with black, ginger and white markings. And there were her three babies, snuffling around in the hay and squeaking. Two of them had similar markings to Carla, while the other had a ruffled, black coat. "Oh, they're gorgeous!" Mandy breathed.

"I know," Lisa said proudly.

"Is it still all right for Lisa to come to tea at your house tonight, Mandy?" Mrs Glover called from the driver's seat.

"Oh, yes." Mandy nodded enthusiastically. "My mum and dad are really looking forward to seeing Carla's babies!"

Mandy and Lisa went off to their classroom,

where everyone was waiting impatiently for them.

"Now keep quiet," Mrs Todd instructed the class, as they gathered round the cage. "Remember that they're still quite young. How old are they exactly, Lisa?"

"They're nearly four weeks," Lisa replied. "And they were born with all their fur and their teeth, and their eyes were open."

"Wow!" said Richard Tanner admiringly. "That's very different to kittens, isn't it, Mrs Todd?" Richard's Persian cat, Duchess, had had three kittens not long ago.

"Tell us their names, Lisa," Mandy said, smiling as the baby guinea-pigs scuttled round the cage, squeaking.

"That's Candy, and that's Mabel," Lisa said, pointing out the two babies who were the same colours as Carla. "And the black one is Shadow."

"Why is Shadow's coat all ruffled up like that?" Dillon Lewis asked.

"He's a rosetted guinea-pig," Lisa explained proudly. "Look, the pattern on his fur looks a bit like a rosette."

"Yes, like my Manchester United rosette," Dillon said, turning pink as everyone laughed.

"When do the guinea-pigs go to their new homes, Lisa?" Mrs Todd asked.

"Mum says they have to go in the next few days," Lisa replied. "I'm really going to miss them."

"Have you found owners for them yet?" Mandy asked.

"Candy and Mabel have got new homes to go to," Lisa replied. "But I still have to find one for Shadow."

"I'd like to have Shadow," Richard Tanner said eagerly.

"Me too," added Sally Martin.

"My Ginny would like a friend to play with!" said Pam Stanton. Ginny was Pam's guinea-pig.

Several other people in the class said that *they'd* like to have Shadow too. Mandy was very relieved. It seemed that Shadow was going to have lots of different homes to choose from. For once, it was going to be easy to find a home for an animal who needed one . . .

GUINEA-PIGS GALORE!

* * *

"I don't know what to do!" Lisa groaned. She was sitting in Animal Ark's big, cosy living room with Carla on her lap. "It seems like *everyone* at school wants Shadow!"

"I think there were about *eight* people in my class who said they were going home to ask their mum about it," James said, holding Candy carefully.

"You'll just have to decide who would be the best owner, Lisa," said Mandy, as Mabel perched on her shoulder.

School was over for the day, and Lisa and James had come back to Mandy's house for tea. When Lisa had carried the guinea-pigs out to Mr Hope's Land-rover, almost everyone in the school had stopped her to have a look at them. It seemed that Shadow was going to have lots of different homes to choose from.

"Yes, but *how*?" Lisa looked worried.

"What do you think, Mum?" Mandy turned to Emily Hope, who was sitting on the sofa behind them.

"Why don't you ask the people who want

Shadow to write a letter, saying why they're the best person for the job?" Mandy's mum suggested.

"That's a great idea, Mum," Mandy said eagerly, and Lisa and James nodded. "We could put up a poster on the school noticeboard."

Mandy put Mabel carefully back in the cage. Then she ran to get a piece of paper and some coloured pens, and they all got to work. Soon the poster was ready.

WANTED

A good home and a loving new owner for
SHADOW
Please write a letter saying why you want
this gorgeous guinea-pig! Give your letters to
Lisa Glover, Mandy Hope or James Hunter.
Thank you!

"It looks great," James said, gazing at the poster.

"And I've got a photo of Shadow at home that I can stick underneath," Lisa added.

"You'll soon have a brilliant new home to go to, Shadow!" Mandy said, tickling the rosetted guinea-pig on his head. "I wonder how many letters we'll get?"

"Here you are, Lisa." Mandy handed over a bundle of letters. "Here's five more."

James was running across the playground towards them. "And here's three more from my class."

Lisa added them to the letters in her bag. "I can't believe there're so many!" she said, shaking her head. "Let me count them."

It was the following day. Mandy, James and Lisa had arrived at school early that morning to put up the poster, which had soon drawn an interested crowd. The letters had started pouring in, and they had a large bundle of them by the time the home bell rang. Lisa and James were going to Animal Ark with Mandy to read through the letters, so that they could ask Mr and Mrs Hope's advice about them.

"How many?" James asked eagerly, as Lisa counted the bundle.

"Sixteen," Lisa replied, looking very surprised. "I never expected that many."

"We're bound to find Shadow a good home!" Mandy said happily.

As soon as they got back to the Hopes' cottage, Mandy, James and Lisa gathered round the kitchen table and spread the letters out. Mr Hope was out on afternoon visits, but Mrs Hope was there.

"Mum, will you help us look through the letters?" Mandy asked. Emily Hope nodded.

"I don't think we should choose *this* one," James said, glancing at the first letter. "It says

I really want a guinea-pig, but my mum doesn't like them. So I'd have to keep Shadow hidden in my bedroom."

"Oh, dear," Mrs Hope said. "I think the person who wrote that had better remain nameless!"

Mandy took a handful of the letters, and began looking through them. Most of them were quite good, but it was the third one she read which caught her eye:

Dear Lisa, Mandy and James,
We have been saving up to buy a guinea-pig for four months now, and we would love to be Shadow's new owners. Our parents have said we can have a guinea-pig if we pay for everything out of our pocket-money. We have already bought a book about looking after guinea-pigs, and we have also got loads of information off the internet. We think we would be good owners because there are two of us to look after Shadow, so he would get plenty of attention.
Yours sincerely
Katy and Luke Tatford

Mandy didn't know Katy or Luke very well, because Katy was in Class 6 and Luke was in Class 3, but she thought it was a very good letter. She passed it over to her mum.

"Mum, what do you think?" she asked.

Her mum read it carefully, then gave it to Lisa. "I think Katy and Luke sound like they would be very good owners," Emily Hope replied thoughtfully. "They've done a lot of research into guinea-pigs already."

"And they must want a guinea-pig a lot if they've been saving all this time," added James, who was reading the letter over Lisa's shoulder.

"Yes," Lisa agreed. "And they could share looking after Shadow."

"It looks like we're agreed then," Mandy grinned. "Katy and Luke are Shadow's new owners!"

"I'll tell them tomorrow," Lisa replied, looking pleased.

"I bet they're going to be thrilled!" said James.

The following day was Friday, and Mandy and

James got to school early. They didn't want to miss Lisa telling Katy and Luke the good news about Shadow. Lisa arrived soon after, and they waited impatiently by the gates for Katy and Luke to arrive. There was no sign of them for ages, then two minutes before the bell was due to ring, Mandy spotted them running down the road.

"They're a bit late," James grinned, as Katy and Luke rushed through the gates. They stopped dead when they saw Lisa, and glanced at each other.

"I wanted to talk to you about Shadow," Lisa began, and a big grin spread across Katy and Luke's faces. "We really liked your letter, and—"

"Are we going to be Shadow's new owners?" Luke interrupted, looking so delighted that Mandy and James couldn't help laughing.

"If you still want him," Lisa smiled.

"Of course we do!" Katy said firmly, her eyes shining.

"When can we have him?" Luke wanted to know.

"Well, Mum says the babies have to go their new homes this weekend," Lisa replied.

"Have you got a cage yet?" Mandy asked Katy and Luke.

They shook their heads. "We'd better get one tonight, Katy," Luke said. "We'll ask Mum to take us to the pet shop in Walton after school."

"The cages are quite expensive," Lisa said. "You need a good-sized one for a guinea-pig, and maybe a run in the garden too."

"How much are they?" Katy asked.

"About thirty pounds," Lisa replied. "More, if you want a run in your garden—" She stopped as she saw the look on Katy and Luke's faces.

"We can't afford that, can we, Katy?" Luke looked anxiously at his sister.

"You could always buy a second-hand cage," Mandy suggested. "They're quite a lot cheaper, and it would be OK, as long as it's clean."

"But how are we going to get one by tomorrow?" Luke looked even gloomier.

"Lisa, do you think your mum would let

you keep Shadow for us until we get a second-hand cage?" Katy asked pleadingly.

"I don't know," Lisa said doubtfully. "But I'll ask her."

"OK," said Luke. "And if we can't find a second-hand cage quickly, maybe Mum will lend us the money for a new one."

But Mandy could see that he didn't look too hopeful. Neither did Katy. It looked as if the Tatfords might not be Shadow's new owners after all. It was a real shame . . .

"Thanks for coming with me," Lisa said to Mandy and James, as they walked through Welford to the Tatfords' house the following morning. "Katy and Luke are going to be so upset when I tell them I can't keep Shadow for them."

"Maybe your mum will change her mind," Mandy suggested.

"I don't think so," Lisa sighed. "She's sorry for Katy and Luke, but she says it should be easy to find another owner quickly. After all, we *did* get sixteen letters."

"Do you think Katy and Luke might have found a second-hand cage by now?" James asked hopefully.

"There weren't any for sale in the local paper last night," Mandy replied. "I looked."

The Tatfords lived in a small house near Hobart's Corner. Mandy rang the bell, and Katy answered the door. She looked eagerly at Lisa. "What did your mum say?" she asked.

"I'm sorry," Lisa replied, looking uncomfortable. "She says the babies have to go to their new homes right away."

"Oh." Katy's face fell, as she stood aside to let them in. "We'd better go and tell Luke."

Luke was outside in the Tatfords' back garden. "Hi," he called. "We were just deciding where to put Shadow's cage – when we get it!"

Then he saw Katy shaking her head at him, and his own face fell.

"Don't give up yet," Mandy told him. "Maybe there'll be a cage for sale in tonight's paper."

"Hello there!"

Everyone turned round as a head appeared over the fence between the Tatfords' garden and the one next door. A cheery-faced, elderly lady was beaming at them. She was dressed in old gardening clothes, and was carrying a trowel.

"Hello, Mrs Hayes," Katy said. "These are our friends, Mandy, Lisa and James."

"Pleased to meet you," the old lady replied. "I thought I'd do a bit of gardening, as it's such a nice day. It's a bit of a jungle out here!"

Mandy glanced over the fence at Mrs Hayes' garden. The old lady was right. It *was* very overgrown and full of weeds. It was a lot of work for one person.

"We'll help you, Mrs Hayes," said Mandy. She turned to Katy and Luke. "Won't we?"

"Of course we will," Luke agreed.

They scrambled over the low fence and followed Mrs Hayes to the garden shed to collect some tools.

It was dark inside and very dusty. Mrs Hayes switched on a torch. "Rake, hoe, trowel . . . now where's the spade?" she said, looking puzzled, as she flashed the torch over the objects.

Suddenly Mandy stiffened. What was that she could see in the corner? It was almost hidden by piles of boxes, but it looked like—

"Mrs Hayes," Mandy said breathlessly, "is that a *guinea-pig hutch* down there?"

"Well, it's a rabbit hutch," Mrs Hayes replied, looking surprised. "I used to have a rabbit called Barney."

"Do you still need it?" Mandy asked, as Katy

and Luke glanced at each other in amazed delight. "Because if you don't, I know someone who could use it . . ."

Quickly Mandy explained about Shadow.

"Why, of course you can have the hutch!" Mrs Hayes said generously. "After all, you've offered to help me with the gardening – one good turn deserves another. It'll need cleaning though."

"We don't mind," Katy said happily. "Thanks very much, Mrs Hayes!"

"You'd better get it out and have a look at it first," the old lady suggested.

Mandy and Lisa dragged the cage outside into the light. It was in quite good condition, and it was very roomy. Mandy thought it would be perfect.

Luke and Katy's dad carried the cage round to the Tatfords' garden, and Mandy, James, Katy and Luke gave it a good clean. Mrs Hayes came round too, to give them a hand. Meanwhile, Lisa went home to fetch Shadow.

"I can't believe that cage was sitting next

door all the time!" Luke said, scrubbing away at the sleeping area.

"We'll have to go shopping straightaway, and buy a water-bottle and some food and some bedding," Katy said to Luke. Lisa had said she would bring some hay, so that Shadow would have some bedding to begin with.

"It's a cage fit for a guinea-pig king!" Mandy said, when everything was clean and scrubbed.

"Here's Lisa and Shadow now!" Luke could hardly stand still, he was so excited.

Everyone gathered round, as Lisa brought Shadow into the garden in his carrying-box. Quickly Mandy took the hay Lisa had brought, and spread it out in the sleeping-compartment. Then Lisa handed Shadow to Katy and Luke. "He's yours now!" she smiled.

Beaming, Katy and Luke gently opened the box, and let Shadow run into his new home. The baby guinea-pig sniffed the air, then began to explore. He ran around every inch of the cage, and then gave a loud squeak as if to say *I love it!*

Mrs Hayes looked delighted. "It *is* nice to

see a pet in the old hutch again," she said. "I hope you'll let me come and visit Shadow sometimes."

"Of course we will," said Katy and Luke together.

"You might have had to say goodbye to your mum and sisters, Shadow, but you've got a new family right here," Mandy laughed, stroking the excited guinea-pig's head. "Welcome home!"

Disappearing Act

"Mandy, I'm going over to Westmoor House," Mrs Hope called from the kitchen. "Are you coming with me or not?"

"You bet!" Mandy Hope shouted back. She flew down the stairs, buttoning her jacket at the same time. "I haven't seen the kittens for *ages*."

"I mustn't forget those eardrops for Sam," said Mrs Hope, as she checked through her medical bag. "Mandy, pop into the surgery and get them for me, will you? They're on Jean's desk."

Mandy nodded, and hurried through the kitchen into the modern extension that was Animal Ark's veterinary surgery. Sam was one of the six kittens who lived at Westmoor House, the old people's home just outside Welford. Mandy picked up the bottle of eardrops from the receptionist's desk, and went back to her mum. "Sam's ear infection isn't serious, is it?" she asked anxiously.

"Not really," Emily Hope replied, putting on her coat. "But the other drops I got for him didn't work. These are stronger, so they should do the trick."

"Oh, good," Mandy said, relieved. She was very fond of Sam, and of Clown, Cheeky, Ginger, Carrots and George, the other kittens who lived at Westmoor House. The kittens had been homeless and unwanted until Mandy had had the brainwave of offering them to the elderly residents of Westmoor House as "pat-cats". Mandy's grandad had seen a TV programme about dogs being taken into hospitals and homes. When the patients and residents stroked the dogs, it made them feel better. Mandy had thought it was a brilliant idea and had suggested they do the same with the kittens. Now the kittens had a permanent home at Westmoor House where they were adored by everyone, including the home's manager, Della Skilton.

"I wonder how the kittens are getting on," Mandy said eagerly, as they drove through Welford. "Last time I went to visit, Clown climbed right to the top of the sitting-room curtains, and wouldn't come down!"

"Yes, he likes climbing, doesn't he!" Emily Hope said, glancing sideways at Mandy.

Mandy turned pink. Her mum was teasing her. Clown, who was black and ginger, was by far the naughtiest of the six kittens. On the day that the kittens were due to arrive at Westmoor House, he'd escaped from the cat basket and got stuck up a nearby tree. Mandy had climbed up to rescue him herself, and her mum hadn't been too pleased at the time.

"Oh, look," Mandy said, as they turned into

the drive of Westmoor House, "the mobile library's here."

The large van, which had come from the main library in the nearby town of Walton, was parked in front of the big Victorian building. It was clearly very popular with the residents, because there were lots of them queuing up to get in. The van doors were open, and Mandy could see racks and racks of books lining the walls.

At the front was a tiny desk where Peggy, the librarian, checked the books in and out. She was very busy, but she spotted Mandy and her mum getting out of the car and waved. "Hello, Mrs Hope, hello, Mandy!" she called. "Are you here to see the kittens?"

"That's right," Mandy called back.

Some of the residents turned round too, and waved.

"That's the girl who gave us those lovely pat-cats," Mandy heard one elderly lady say to another, and she couldn't help feeling quite proud.

"Don't forget you've got some books to

return to the mobile library today, Mandy," her mum reminded her, as she lifted her bag out of the car.

Mandy nodded. She'd borrowed a really fantastic book of cat stories, and an information book about animals of the rainforest. She'd return them this afternoon when Peggy and the mobile library stopped at Welford village green.

As Mandy and her mum walked towards the front door of Westmoor House, an elderly man hurried out, clutching a pile of library books. A black-and-ginger kitten was perched on his shoulder, looking quite at home.

Mandy laughed. "Hello, George," she said. Then she reached up and scratched the kitten's silky head. "And hello, George the Second!"

"I want to change my library books in peace," George grumbled. "But this pesky little thing won't leave me alone!" His eyes were twinkling, though. Meanwhile, George the kitten was purring contentedly, and rubbing his head against the other George's ear.

Mandy grinned. She'd named the kitten after

the old man because he was one of the residents who'd objected to the pat-cats when they'd voted whether to have the kittens or not. Mandy had hoped that it might make George like the kittens more if one had the same name as him – and it had worked! Now the two Georges were best friends.

"Oh, Emily, Mandy, hello." Della Skilton rushed into the hallway with a sheaf of papers in her hand, as Mandy and her mum walked in. "Have you come to check up on Sam?"

Emily Hope nodded. "I've brought the eardrops I was telling you about on the phone."

"Oh, good," said Della, looking relieved. "The residents have been very worried about him. His ear really is very sore, poor thing."

"Where is he?" Mandy asked anxiously.

"Dolly's looking after him in her room," Della replied. Dolly was one of the residents who'd been very keen to have the pat-cats right from the start. "We've kept him away from the other kittens in case they catch it too."

"Good idea," said Mrs Hope approvingly. "I'd better take a look at him."

"You know where Dolly's room is, don't you?" Della asked, and Mandy and her mum nodded.

They hurried down the corridor towards Dolly's room, and Mandy sneaked a quick peek into the residents' sitting room as they went by.

Ginger, the laziest kitten in the litter, was stretched out on an old man's lap, having a snooze in the sun. The man was fast asleep too. The oldest kitten, Cheeky, was playing with a ball of wool which was being dangled for him by Mrs Brown, who was one hundred years old, and the oldest resident in the home. And Carrots was chasing sunbeams round the room, while some of the elderly residents watched him and laughed.

"I wonder where Clown is," Mandy said, as they went on down the corridor. She was longing to go into the sitting room and say hello to the other kittens, but it was important that they saw Sam first.

"Probably off somewhere causing mischief!" Mrs Hope remarked. "Ah, here's Dolly's room."

Dolly was waiting in the doorway, looking out for them anxiously. Meanwhile, Sam was curled up in a basket in one corner of the sunny, airy bedroom. He looked rather glum.

"Oh, poor Sam!" Mandy said. At the sound of her voice, Sam climbed to his feet and mewed pathetically.

"He's a bit under the weather, Mrs Hope," Dolly explained, as Mandy's mum picked the kitten up.

"The infection's probably making him feel quite low," Mrs Hope said, examining the kitten's ear. "Just give him the eardrops at regular intervals, and he should be as right as rain in a few days' time."

Just then they heard the sound of footsteps hurrying down the corridor. A moment later Tom, one of the other residents, put his head round Dolly's door.

"Dolly, have you seen Clown?" he asked, looking worried. Then he spotted Mandy and her mum. "Oh, hello."

"Hello, Tom." Mandy smiled at the old man.

Along with George, Tom had been the other resident to object to the pat-cats, but now Clown had become his best friend. "What's happened to Clown?"

"I don't know." Tom looked even more worried. "I gave him his breakfast this morning, but one minute he was here – and the next he was gone!"

"Typical!" Dolly snorted, but she was

smiling. "That cat's got his nose into *everything*. Last week he climbed into the washing-machine, and yesterday I walked into the bathroom, and found him sitting in the bath! He'll be around somewhere."

But Tom still didn't look very happy. "Clown's gone missing before, and I've always found him in the grounds," he muttered. "But I've looked all round the gardens, and I can't see him anywhere."

Mandy felt very sorry for Tom, as well as worried about Clown. "Shall I help you to look round the home again?" she suggested.

But Tom shook his head. "He's not inside, I'm sure of it," he said. "I've been round shaking a packet of kitten biscuits. Clown *always* comes for biscuits."

"I hope Clown hasn't managed to get out of the grounds somehow," Mandy said anxiously. Then she wished she hadn't said it because Tom looked even gloomier.

"I'm sure he'll turn up sooner or later," Emily Hope said gently. "Try not to worry too much, Tom."

"And I'll look for him on our way out," Mandy promised.

Tom nodded and tried to smile, but Mandy knew that he wouldn't stop worrying until Clown was found. *If* he was found . . .

"Poor Tom," Mandy sighed, as she and James Hunter walked through Welford, their arms full of books. It was the middle of the afternoon, and they were on their way to Welford village green to visit the mobile library. "I hope he's found Clown by now."

"Perhaps we could go and help him look after we've been to the library," James said eagerly. He was Mandy's best friend, and he loved animals as much as she did. "Do you think your mum would take us over to Westmoor House when afternoon surgery's finished?"

"We'll ask her," Mandy replied, cheering up a little. She'd hardly been able to eat any lunch, she was so worried about the lost kitten.

"Maybe Blackie could help us," James suggested, looking down at his black Labrador puppy who was trotting along the path on his lead. "Remember when the kittens escaped from their basket before? Blackie helped us to find some of them."

Mandy nodded.

"And Blackie's a lot more sensible now," James went on. "He's not as naughty as he used to be – *Blackie*! Stop that!"

Blackie had just spotted a man on a bike cycling past, and chased after him, dragging James along the pavement.

"Blackie! I nearly dropped my library books in that puddle!" James said sternly, as he managed to get the puppy under control at last. Blackie wagged his tail furiously, looking very pleased with himself, as he tried to lick James's hand.

The mobile library was parked at the side of the village green, its doors wide open. Mandy, James and Blackie went over to it, but as they did so, something strange happened. Mrs McFarlane, who ran the post office in Welford, suddenly rushed down the steps, with Peggy the librarian close behind her. They both looked rather scared.

"Are you all right, Peggy?" Mandy asked.

Both women jumped. "Oh, I didn't see you there, Mandy," Peggy said distractedly.

Mrs McFarlane was breathing rather hard. "Don't let Mandy and James go in there," she said to the librarian. "Not until you know what's making that noise!"

"What noise?" James asked curiously. "Blackie, be quiet!"

The Labrador puppy was going mad, barking his head off and trying to pull James up the steps and into the van. In desperation, James took Blackie over to a nearby bench, and tied him firmly to it, out of the way.

"Tell us about the noise, Mrs McFarlane," Mandy said, when James had come back.

"Well . . . " Mrs McFarlane glanced fearfully over her shoulder at the van. "I went in to change my library book, and I heard this sort of ghostly, wailing noise. Peggy heard it too."

Peggy nodded. "I've got no idea what it was," she murmured. "But it sounded *horrible*."

James nudged Mandy. "I've never heard of a haunted mobile library!" he whispered.

"Me neither," Mandy whispered back. Then her eyes widened. "Listen, James!"

Awoooooh! Awoooooh! The muffled wailing sound was indeed coming from the van. Mandy couldn't help feeling a bit scared too. What on earth could it be? Even James looked a bit spooked.

"See?" said Mrs McFarlane, with a shiver. "And there's nothing in there at all!"

They all peered into the empty van.

Then Mandy clutched James's arm so hard, she made him jump. "I think it's coming from behind the shelves," she whispered.

They all listened hard. And sure enough, when the wailing noise started again, it *was* coming from behind the shelves.

"It's coming from over there," Mandy said, pointing at the *Pets* section.

James was looking puzzled. "It sounds like a cat," he remarked. "I've heard Benji make a noise like that sometimes." Benji was the Hunters' big, fluffy cat.

"A cat?" Mandy repeated. Then she gasped. "Clown!"

"Be careful, Mandy," Mrs McFarlane shouted anxiously, as Mandy dashed up the steps and into the van.

"Peggy, we need to take the books off the shelves," Mandy called, as the librarian and James followed her inside. "Is that OK?"

Peggy nodded, and the three of them set to work. Soon they had half the books in the *Pets* section cleared off the shelves. The wailing noise was getting louder, and now they could hear the sound of frantic scratching too.

"Clown!" Mandy called softly. "Is that you?"

At that moment a dusty, furry little head popped into view from behind a shelf. "Miaow!" Clown said happily, as if to say *Here I am*!

Mandy scooped up the kitten, and gave him a hug. "Thank goodness you're safe, Clown!" she sighed.

"So *that's* why Blackie was making such a fuss when we arrived," James remembered. "He must have smelled Clown in the van."

"Clown must have sneaked in when I was up at Westmoor House this morning," Peggy smiled. "And then he crawled behind the shelves and got stuck, the little scamp."

"He was in the right section though!" James grinned, pointing at the label, which said *Pets*.

They all laughed, even Mrs McFarlane, who had joined them in the van once she'd realised it wasn't a ghost.

"Come on, Clown." Mandy settled the kitten more firmly in her arms. "It's time to take you home."

"Look, there's Tom," Mandy said, as her mum turned the car into the drive of Westmoor House. The elderly man was walking slowly up and down outside the home, shaking a packet of cat biscuits, and glancing from side to side. "He's still searching for Clown."

The black and ginger kitten, who was sitting on Mandy's lap in the passenger seat, sat up straight, and began to purr.

"Tom's going to be so pleased when he knows we've found Clown!" James said happily. He was in the back seat, along with Blackie.

"He's certainly a very lucky little kitten," Emily Hope remarked, as she drew to a halt outside the home. "He could have ended up miles from Welford!"

Tom had spotted the car, and was coming over to them. He looked very depressed.

Smiling all over her face, Mandy held Clown up to the window. "Look, Tom!" she cried. "We found him! We found Clown!"

Tom's face lit up with delight, and he rushed over to the car. Meanwhile, Clown had seen him too, and was purring his very loudest, scratching at the window to try and get out to greet his friend.

Next moment, Tom had the kitten in his arms, and was hugging him tightly. "Clown, I thought you were never coming home!" he murmured, burying his face in the kitten's black-and-ginger fur. Clown purred, rubbed his furry cheek against Tom's, and then tried to stick his head through the hole in the packet of cat biscuits.

Tom looked at Mandy, and beamed at her. "Thank you so much, Mandy," he said. "Wherever did you find him?"

"Well, did you know that Clown just *loves* to read, Tom?" Mandy asked. Tom looked puzzled. Mandy and James glanced at each other and laughed. "We'll tell you all about it," Mandy smiled. "But it all began the day the mobile library came to Westmoor House . . ."

A Very Special Mother

"Why are we going to Blackheath Farm, Dad?" Mandy asked, as her father turned off the main road and drove up the bumpy track.

"Well, one of the new hens, Marjorie, is off her food," her father replied. "And she's also losing her feathers."

"Oh dear," Mandy said anxiously. "Mr Masters will be really upset — he takes such good care of all his animals."

"I'm hoping that there won't be anything

seriously wrong," Mr Hope replied, as he drove through the open gates which led into the farmyard. "Look, there's Libby."

Mandy smiled as she saw Libby Masters standing in the doorway of the farmhouse, waving at them. She knew the dark-haired girl from Welford Primary School where she was in Class 1. Mandy had taken care of the little girl when she'd first arrived in the area.

Libby rushed over as Mandy and her dad climbed out of the car. "Hello, Mandy, hello, Mr Hope," she said breathlessly. "Dad's with Marjorie. He asked me to take you straight over there."

"How is Marjorie?" Mandy asked, as Libby led them quickly across the farmyard, past a large pen full of hens who were wandering about, clucking happily and scratching around in the earth.

"She's not eating properly," Libby said worriedly. "Dad thinks she might have something wrong with her tummy."

"It's a possibility," Mr Hope agreed.

"Dad's keeping Marjorie away from the other

chickens, just in case they catch whatever she's got," Libby said, as they went past the other henhouses. "We've had to move her chicks into the barn as well."

"Oh, has Marjorie had chicks?" said Mandy, delighted. She loved seeing the fluffy, yellow, newborn babies.

Libby nodded. "Yes, she had eleven chicks two weeks ago. You can come and see them later if you want to. They're in a pen in the barn."

"I'd love to," Mandy said eagerly. "By the way, Libby, how's Ronda?" Ronda was Libby's own pet hen.

"Oh, she's fine," Libby said happily. "She's scratching around somewhere."

"I'll say hello to her later," Mandy promised.

Libby stopped outside one of the henhouses which stood on its own, a little further away from the others. "Marjorie's in here, Mr Hope," she said.

Mandy was just about to follow Libby and her father into the henhouse, when her attention was caught by something else. She

had just spotted a black-and-white sheepdog sniffing its way around the edge of the farmyard. Mandy was very surprised. Mr Masters was a chicken farmer, so he didn't need a sheepdog at all. And Mandy knew that the Masters' family didn't have a pet dog either. So where had it come from?

"Here, girl," Mandy called softly, walking forward slowly with her hand held out in front of her. "Where have you come from then? Good dog!"

The sheepdog froze, lifted her head and stared

nervously at Mandy for a few seconds. Then she turned, and ran off round the side of the barn, her long tail swishing from side to side.

Mandy frowned, as she went into the henhouse. She hoped the poor dog wasn't a stray. She decided to ask Libby and Mr Masters if they knew anything about her.

Mandy's dad had just begun examining Marjorie when Mandy joined them. Mr Masters smiled at her, even though he seemed worried. "Hello, Mandy," he said. "How are you?"

"Fine, thank you, Mr Masters," Mandy replied, staring at Marjorie. The poor hen really did look miserable. She'd lost quite a few white feathers from her head and from the black ruff around her neck, and she was looking a bit thin and sickly. "What's the matter with her, Dad?" Mandy asked.

"I'm not quite sure." Mr Hope frowned. "I'm going to have to give her a thorough examination."

"Why don't you take Mandy to see Marjorie's chicks, Libby?" Mr Masters suggested. "You can always come back in a little while to find out how Marjorie is."

"OK," Libby agreed.

"Mr Masters, I saw a sheepdog in the yard just now," Mandy said quickly, not wanting to leave until she'd found out something about the mysterious dog. "Do you know where she's come from?"

Mr Masters' face darkened. "So that dog's hanging around again, is it? I've seen it a few times, and I've tried to shoo it away. I don't want it going after my chickens."

"So you don't know who she belongs to?" Mandy asked.

Mr Masters shook his head. "If you find out, let me know," he muttered. "I want that dog off my land."

"Have *you* seen the dog, Libby?" Mandy asked, as the two of them left the henhouse, and went over to the barn.

"Yes, I have," Libby replied. "I tried calling her, but she wouldn't come to me."

Mandy didn't say any more, but she was determined to help the stray dog, if she could.

She didn't *look* like a stray, Mandy thought, feeling rather puzzled. Her coat was quite clean and glossy, and she didn't look thin and underfed. Mandy frowned. It was a bit of a mystery.

The chicks were running about in their low-walled pen inside the barn, looking like fluffy balls of yellow wool on legs.

Mandy grinned at Libby. "They're gorgeous!" she said. "Can we hold them?"

"Sure," Libby replied, opening the pen door.

Mandy scooped up a tiny chick and held it in her hand, loving the feel of its soft, downy feathers against her skin. The chick seemed quite happy to be held, and cheeped loudly.

Mandy laughed, as she put him back gently with his brothers and sisters. "I hope they all grow up to be as beautiful as their mum!" she said. "Don't worry, Libby. I'm sure Marjorie will be fine."

"We'd better go back and see how she is," said Libby, putting down the chick she was holding. "Your dad might have found out

what's wrong with her by now."

"OK," Mandy agreed.

"I'll just go and see if I can find Ronda," said Libby, as they left the barn. "She'd love to say hello to you!"

Mandy nodded, and went back to the henhouse on her own. Her father had finished examining Marjorie, and was talking to Mr Masters. "Is Marjorie going to be OK, Dad?" Mandy asked anxiously.

"Yes, I think so," Mr Hope replied. "She *has* got something wrong with her digestive system – her tummy – but I think some antibiotics in her food or water will fix it."

"Oh, good," Mandy said, relieved. Marjorie was back in her nest, hunched up and still looking glum. "Did you hear that, Marjorie? You'll be all right soon!"

"Thanks very much, Adam," Mr Masters said, shaking Mr Hope by the hand.

Suddenly Libby rushed into the henhouse. She was shaking, and tears were pouring down her face. Everyone stared at her.

"Libby, what's wrong?" Mandy cried.

"I was looking for Ronda, and I went past the barn, and I saw that the chicks were gone!" Libby gulped. "I can't have closed the door of the pen properly!"

Mr Masters turned pale. "Oh no, what about that dog?" he gasped, and dashed out of the henhouse.

Mandy and Mr Hope followed close behind him. Mandy's heart was thumping loudly. "Oh, *please* let the chicks be all right!" she breathed.

Libby was still crying, so Mandy took the younger girl's hand. "Come on, Libby," she said, trying to sound cheerful, "We'll look for them together. I bet we'll find them really quickly."

They all began to search the farmyard. There was no sign of the sheepdog, but there was no sign of the chicks either. They seemed to have vanished into thin air.

"Oh, where *are* they?" Libby began to cry again.

"They must be *somewhere*," Mandy said anxiously to her father.

Suddenly Mr Masters came out of the barn,

looking rather dazed. "Come here," he called. "Quick!"

Mandy, Libby and Mr Hope rushed over to the barn. Mandy peeped inside, and could hardly believe what she was seeing. All eleven chicks were back in their pen, and, lying across the entrance to keep them in, was the stray sheepdog!

"That dog must have rounded them all up and put them back in the pen!" Mr Masters said, scratching his head in disbelief. "I don't believe it!"

Mandy smiled, as a very bold chick climbed up on to the sheepdog's shoulder, and was gently but firmly pushed back into the pen by the dog's nose. "Good dog!" she said.

The sheepdog looked at her and wagged her feathery tail, but didn't move from her post in front of the pen.

"Well, well, this dog isn't after my chicks at all," Mr Masters said, looking very relieved. "In fact, she's been a great help!"

"I've heard about female sheepdogs adopting chicks before," said Adam Hope, squatting down next to the dog. "But that was when they'd had pups of their own. I wonder if she's had a litter recently . . ."

Mandy watched as her father examined the dog, who didn't seem to mind at all.

"Yes, I'd say she's had pups a couple of months ago," he said at last.

"Maybe she's missing them," Mandy suggested. "That could be why she's looking after the chicks."

"Could be," her dad agreed.

"But where has she come from?" Libby asked. "She hasn't got a collar or anything."

"Dad!" Mandy said excitedly, as an idea suddenly popped into her head. "Do you think Dora Janeki at Syke Farm might know who the dog belongs to? After all, she's a sheep farmer."

"And she probably knows all the other sheep farmers and their dogs in the district," Adam Hope said thoughtfully. "Good idea, Mandy."

"You can use the phone in the farmhouse," Mr Masters said, and the two men went out.

"Oh, I hope they find out who the dog belongs to," Libby said.

"Me too," Mandy agreed, gently stroking the dog's silky ears. She just hoped the sheepdog had a loving home waiting for her. If she didn't, it would be up to Mandy to find her one!

Mr Hope and Mr Masters came back after a few minutes. They were both smiling.

"Dad, did you find out anything?" Mandy cried.

"We certainly did," her father replied. "Dora said that her neighbours, the Clays at Hilltop Farm, have a sheepdog called Fly which had puppies a few months ago. The dog actually belongs to Darren, who's the son of Mr and Mrs Clay."

"So do you think Fly ran away from Hilltop Farm?" Mandy asked, smiling as the dog's tail began to wag frantically on hearing its name.

Mr Hope nodded. "Looks like it. We rang the Clays next, and they said she'd been missing for a few days. They didn't say why, though. But we can ask Darren. He's coming to collect her right away."

Mandy couldn't help feeling worried. Perhaps Fly had run away from the Clays because they didn't look after her properly, or they were unkind to her . . .

Darren Clay arrived about half an hour later. He was a young man in his twenties with untidy dark hair, and he was still wearing his muddy work clothes and boots.

Looking excited, he rushed over to the barn, where Mandy and the others were standing in the doorway. "Where's Fly?" he asked anxiously.

Mandy smiled as she watched the sheepdog jump up and stand at the entrance to the chick pen, wagging her tail madly from side to side. Fly wasn't going to leave her post, but Mandy could see that every muscle in the dog's body was straining to run towards her owner. It was obvious that they loved each other dearly.

"Fly!" Darren hurried over to the dog, and flung his arms round her. "I've been looking for you everywhere!" Behind them the chicks cheeped happily, as if they were cheering.

"Why did Fly run away from Hilltop Farm in the first place, Darren?" Mr Hope asked curiously.

"We think it was because she missed her pups after we sold them," Darren explained, one arm still round Fly's furry neck. "She moped around the farm, and then one day she just disappeared. She loves being a mum!"

"We can see that!" Mandy laughed. "She rounded up all Marjorie's chicks when they got out!"

"She did?" Darren looked thoughtful. He glanced at the chicks, and then at Libby's dad. "Would you consider selling me the chicks, Mr Masters?"

113

Mr Masters looked a bit surprised.

"I know my mum would like some hens around the place to supply us with eggs," Darren explained. "And it would be good for Fly, too. She'd have something to mother!"

Mr Masters thought for a moment. "Well, I don't see why not," he said at last. "I'm sure we can agree a fair price."

"Great!" Darren said, and the two men shook hands.

Libby beamed at Mandy. "I'll miss the chicks, but at least I know they're going to a good home," she said.

"And they've got a very special new mother too," Mandy added, bending down to give Fly a hug.

FROG FRIENDS
Animal Ark Pets 15

Lucy Daniels

The frogs that come to Farmer Jessop's pond
every spring to lay their spawn have turned
up to find it has been filled in! Another pond
must be found for the frogs if their tadpoles
are to survive. Mandy suggests that the school
pond would make a perfect new home. But
will the frogs agree?

HEDGEHOG HOME
Animal Ark Pets 14

Lucy Daniels

Gran and Grandad Hope are looking after a friend's house over the winter. After a freezing night Mandy and Grandad discover a burst water pipe. And, out in the garden, the flood has destroyed Harold the hedgehog's nest. The garden is too frozen and snowy for Harold to build another home. Can Mandy find him a new one?

Another Hodder Children's book

FERRET FUN
Animal Ark Pets 17

Lucy Daniels

Freddie, a stray ferret, is found under the shed at Lilac Cottage. To make Freddie feel at home, Mandy comes up with a way to include her in a school Fun Day to raise money for new story books. But then Freddie goes missing. Will she turn up in time for the ferret fun?

Another Hodder Children's book

RAT RIDDLE
Animal Ark Pets 18

Lucy Daniels

Mandy and James's schoolfriend Martin has been given a pair of fancy rats for his birthday. Cheddar and Pickle love to race around their incredible 'Rat Run'. At first Mandy finds that Pickle is the fastest. But then Pickle's times begin to slow down. Could something be wrong?

FOAL FROLICS
Animal Ark Pets Summer Special

Lucy Daniels

Mandy and James are on holiday with Mandy's family. All sorts of things are disappearing from the campsite, and now golf balls from the nearby golf course are going missing too. It's a mystery until Mandy and James catch the thief red-handed: a cheeky foal called Mischief! The bad-tempered groundsman at the golf course wants Mischief removed. Can Mandy and James find a way for the foal to stay?

PIGLET PRANKS
Animal Ark Pets Summer Special

Lucy Daniels

The Hopes and James are visiting Mandy's relations in Scotland, and everyone is really excited about the Highland Games! Mandy's cousin Claire is in a dance competition, and Claire's friend Ewan is entering his adorable piglet, Twiglet, in the pets show. Mandy thinks Twiglet is so cute, he has to win! But Twiglet has a rival: Polly, the 'perfect piglet' might steal the show, especially if naughty Twiglet doesn't behave himself!

SPANIEL SURPRISE
Animal Ark Pets Christmas Special

Lucy Daniels

Mandy and James know how much little Ben Harwick wants a dog – it's all he can talk about from morning to night! Ben watches *Give a Dog a Home* on TV every week, and he's desperate to adopt one of the dogs on the show. The trouble is, Ben's mum doesn't seem to like dogs at all – she's being very fussy about the type of dog she wants, and poor Ben is in despair. But with Mandy's help, Ben's mum might just come round to the idea, and Ben could get his dream dog, after all . . .

LUCY DANIELS
Animal Ark Pets

0 340 67283 8	Puppy Puzzle	£3.50	❒
0 340 67284 6	Kitten Crowd	£3.50	❒
0 340 67285 4	Rabbit Race	£3.50	❒
0 340 67286 2	Hamster Hotel	£3.50	❒
0 340 68729 0	Mouse Magic	£3.50	❒
0 340 68730 4	Chick Challenge	£3.50	❒
0 340 68731 2	Pony Parade	£3.50	❒
0 340 68732 0	Guinea-pig Gang	£3.50	❒
0 340 71371 2	Gerbil Genius	£3.50	❒
0 340 71372 0	Duckling Diary	£3.50	❒
0 340 71373 9	Lamb Lessons	£3.50	❒
0 340 71374 7	Doggy Dare	£3.50	❒
0 340 73585 6	Donkey Derby	£3.50	❒
0 340 73586 4	Hedgehog Home	£3.50	❒
0 340 73587 2	Frog Friends	£3.50	❒
0 340 73588 0	Bunny Bonanza	£3.50	❒
0 340 73589 9	Ferret Fun	£3.50	❒
0 340 73590 2	Rat Riddle	£3.50	❒
0 340 71375 5	Cat Crazy	£3.50	❒
0 340 73605 4	Pets' Party	£3.50	❒
0 340 77861 X	Piglet Pranks	£3.50	❒
0 340 77878 4	Spaniel Surprise	£3.50	❒

All Hodder Children's books are available at your local bookshop, or can be ordered direct from the publisher. Just tick the titles you would like and complete the details below. Prices and availability are subject to change without prior notice.

Please enclose a cheque or postal order made payable to *Bookpoint Ltd*, and send to: Hodder Children's Books, 39 Milton Park, Abingdon, OXON OX14 4TD, UK. Email Address: orders@bookpoint.co.uk

If you would prefer to pay by credit card, our call centre team would be delighted to take your order by telephone. Our direct line *01235 400414* (lines open 9.00 am–6.00 pm Monday to Saturday, 24 hour message answering service). Alternatively you can send a fax on *01235 400454*.

TITLE		FIRST NAME		SURNAME	

ADDRESS	

DAYTIME TEL:		POST CODE	

If you would prefer to pay by credit card, please complete:
Please debit my Visa/Access/Diner's Card/American Express (delete as applicable) card no:

Signature .... Expiry Date: ....

If you would NOT like to receive further information on our products please tick the box. ❒